CBeebies
BBC

My Bedtime
Treasury

CBeebies
BBC

My Bedtime
Treasury

My Bedtime Treasury

CONTENTS:

BOB THE BUILDER: Bob's Bucket.......................11

FIMBLES: Snowflake........................35

PINGU: Pingu's Bouncy Fun............59

CONTENTS:

TWEENIES: Dancing Feet.....................83

LITTLE ROBOTS: Rock-A-Bye Robot............107

RUBBADUBBERS: Train Driver Tubb..............131

Bob's
Bucket

"**Dum-de-dum**," Bob hummed, as he put some water in his favourite bucket.
"Oh no!" he said, looking down at his wet feet.
"There's a hole in your bucket!" giggled Wendy. "Here, use this new one."

"Aw," said Bob, "but I've had this bucket for years!"

"Why don't you just throw it away?" said Wendy.

"There must be something else we can use it for," said Bob.

"It would make a great bongo drum," suggested Scoop.

"One bongo drum coming up," said Bob, turning the bucket over and tapping it with his hands.

"**Yahoo!**" called Scoop. "Play it again, Bob!" said Wendy, clapping.

"OK," said Bob, and he beat
out such a good tune that
Wendy and Scoop joined in,
clapping and tapping.

Boom-diddy-boom-boom!

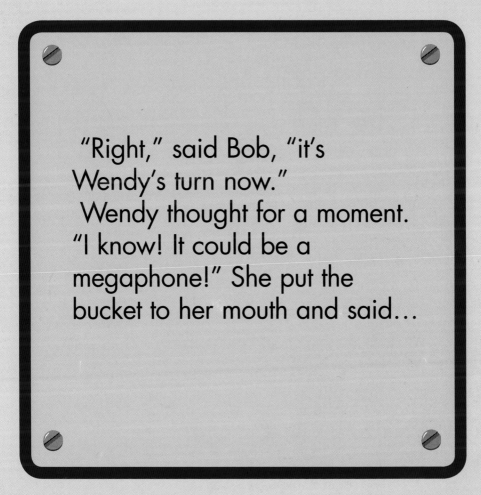

"Right," said Bob, "it's Wendy's turn now."
Wendy thought for a moment. "I know! It could be a megaphone!" She put the bucket to her mouth and said...

"**Calling Roley and Dizzy!**"
Wendy's voice was much
louder than usual. Roley and
Dizzy could hear her right
from the other side of the yard.
They hurried over to see what
she wanted.

"What else could it be,
Wendy?" asked Dizzy.
"Let's see," Wendy said,
as she lifted the bucket close
to her eye. "It would make
a great…"

"…telescope!" she said, "I spy… with my little eye… something beginning with 'b'." Everyone looked up to where the telescope was pointing.

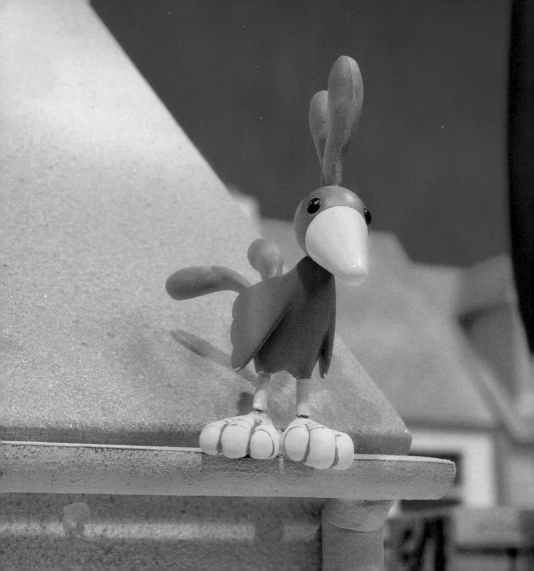

"Roof!" said Roley.
"That doesn't begin with 'b',"
said Bob, laughing.
"I know, but it's the first
letter of my name,"
replied Roley.
"It's Bird!" said Dizzy.

"Well done!" said Wendy, as Roley went to have a closer look.

"Roley – watch out!" called Bob. "You're going to roll over my old…"

"Bucket," said Wendy, but Roley didn't hear her.

"You've squashed my bongo drum!" said Bob.

"And my megaphone," said Wendy, "and my telescope!"

"I didn't realize I was so good at my job," said Roley, "...with one roll I squashed three things as flat as a pancake!"

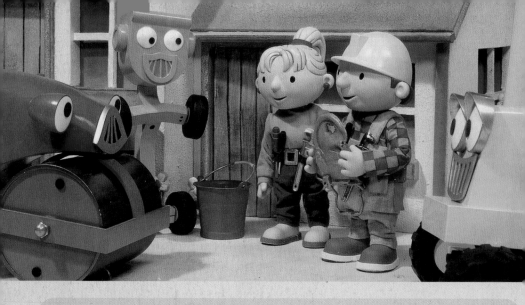

"Four things," moaned Bob, "don't forget my bucket."

"Are you ready to throw it away now?" Wendy asked.

"I suppose so," said Bob, and everyone laughed.

The End

Snowflake

Florrie was busy pulling out all the sparkly things from the busy box.

"Look, Pom," she said, "tinsel! What shall I make today?"

But Baby Pom ran off
without answering.
She was busy getting
the Fimbling Feeling.

"I can feel a twinkling,
I can hear a sound,
It's telling me there's something
Waiting to be found!
Where is it? Where is it?
What could it be?
I think it might be over there,
Let's go and see!"

Baby Pom looked up and saw
something spinning

down,

down,

down,

towards her.

"Oooh," she said, putting out her hand to catch it.
"Shiny! Sparkly! Pom catch it!"

Just then, Fimbo came along.
"What have you caught?" he asked.

But when Baby Pom opened
her hand, the shiny, sparkly
thing had gone.

"It's all gone," she said,
then, "Oh, pretty!" as she
caught another one.

Baby Pom ran off to show Florrie.

"Florrie, Florrie, Florrie!" she called. "Pom a Fimbly Find!"

"What have you found?" asked Florrie.

Baby Pom opened her hand but the shiny, sparkly thing had gone.

When the snow stopped falling, Baby Pom felt sad again.

"Shall we make snowflakes that don't melt away?"
asked Florrie.

"Pom like," said Baby Pom.

So Florrie folded and tore a piece of paper, and when she opened it up, there was a snowflake. Baby Pom made snowflakes by tearing her paper into tiny pieces.

Rockit was sitting by the Bubble Fall watching a snowflake
spin down, down, down, until it landed on the end of his nose.

"Glung! Ohh, that tickles," giggled Rockit.

And when Roly Mo pushed his nose out of the ground,
a snowflake landed right on the end of it.
   "Snow!" chuckled Roly Mo.

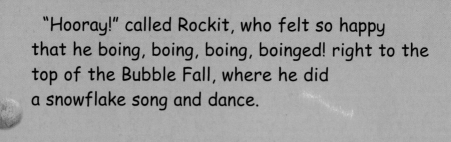

"Hooray!" called Rockit, who felt so happy
that he boing, boing, boing, boinged! right to the
top of the Bubble Fall, where he did
a snowflake song and dance.

The Fimbles were busy
singing and dancing along
when they met Rockit.

And just as Florrie showed
them the paper snowflake...
it stopped snowing.

"All gone," said Baby Pom.

But when she looked up into the sky, a shiny, sparkly snowflake came spinning down, down, down, and it landed on the end of her nose. Baby Pom giggled, and everyone sang the snowflake song over and over again.

The End

Pingu's
Bouncy Fun

Pingu was having fun bouncing on his bed.

But he was making plates
jump off the kitchen shelves.

He wasn't pleased when Mother
told him to stop.

He wanted to keep bouncing.

Mother told him to stay in the living room with Pinga.

But when Pingu
sat in the armchair,
he found it was
really quite bouncy.

Mother heard a noise and came
back in to tell him to stop.

...and bounced on Pinga's rabbit instead.

When Father came home, Mother was glad to take Pinga to the shops.

69

Pingu asked Father to
help him make something he
could bounce on.

They started to collect some
useful things.
The watering can wasn't one
of them!

Gradually, a frame was
starting to take shape.

Father tied on some canvas
and the trampoline
was finished.

Pingu couldn't wait to try it out.
He hopped on...

...and bounced right off
onto the floor.

Pingu tried again.
This time
he bounced...

...right into Father's arms. Father
said he needed more practice.

Mother walked in and wanted to know what they were doing.

**Pingu somersaulted off
the trampoline...**

**...and landed upside down,
in the armchair.**

Father suggested they drag the trampoline outside to play.

Mother gave them each a
crash helmet, to make sure
they were safe.

It was time to BOUNCE!

The End

Tweenies™

Dancing Feet

"Good toes, naughty toes,
good toes, naughty toes," sang Fizz,
as she practised her ballet steps.
Jake tried to copy her but he fell over.

"I'm no good at dancing," he sighed.
"You *just* have to practise," Fizz told him.

"Well, I'll never be a good ballet dancer," said Jake.
"There are lots of other dances you could try,"
Fizz explained. "Let's ask Max about them."

Max showed the Tweenies some dancers on the computer. An Indian girl danced in sparkly clothes, a flamenco dancer from Spain stamped, and a Hungarian dancer wore a hat and slapped his feet.

Jake liked the Greek dance best
danced in a circle.

"Let's dress up and do the dance we each liked best," Fizz suggested. "I'll do the Indian dance."

"I ... dance," said Milo.

"... Bella.

Off they went to dress up, but Jake stayed behind.

"Why don't you try the Greek dance?" Max asked him.

Jake shook his head. He didn't think he danced well enough.

Bella, Milo and Fizz were trying on clothes.

"I'll wear this long, pink scarf," cried Fizz.

Milo found a hat. "Now I look just like a Hungarian dancer," he said.

"I need something frilly," said Bella.

Fizz asked Jake why he wasn't dressing up.

"I'm not good at dancing," Jake told her. "I'll just watch."

The others said they would teach Jake their dances so he

could join in.

At last everyone was ready. Instead of introducing the first dancers, Doodles said, "Meet Dancing Doodles!" and began to dance.

Fizz told him to stop. It was her turn to dance, with Jake.

"Just copy me," Fizz whispered to Jake.

Jake did his best, but he began to feel dizzy.

Doodles didn't introduce the next dancers, either. He started dancing again, until Milo reminded him that it was his and Jake's turn.

"Just follow me," Milo said to Jake. "It's easy."

Milo shouted, "Oi!" and started
dancing and slapping his feet very, very fast.
 "Come on, Jake! Try!" Milo called.
 Jake did his best, but soon he just stopped and watched Milo.

95

"And now it's time for Dancing Doodles," Doodles announced.

"No, it isn't," Bella said firmly. "It's time for Bella and Jake."

"Stand still," Bella told Jake. Then she sang, "Olé!" and stamped round and round Jake until she trod on his foot accidentally. Jake roared, "Owweee!" and limped off to talk to Izzles.

"It's no good," Jake told Izzles. "I tried to dance but I couldn't."

"I'm learning to dance. Watch!" Izzles said. She twirled round a few times and then fell over.

"I need a bit more practise," she panted.

"If I practised, could I do the Greek dance?" Jake asked.

"Of course!" she replied.
"Let's practise it together."

So Jake held out his arms and began
to dance, while Izzles copied him.
"Look, Izzles!" laughed Jake. "I'm dancing!"

99

Bella, Milo and Fizz were wondering what to do.

"Let's do a dance together," Bella suggested.

But they couldn't decide which dance to choose. Milo wanted to teach them his Hungarian dance. Bella thought the flamenco dance would be better. Fizz said they should make up a beautiful Indian dance.

Then someone pressed the surprise time button on the Tweenie clock. The curtains swished open...

...and there was Jake, dressed in a white kilt, with Izzles.

Greek music played and they began to dance.

Everyone clapped and cheered, and when the dance ended they wanted to know how

Jake and Izzles had learnt it.

"I taught myself and Izzles copied me,"
Jake told them. "Then we practised together."

"Come on, everyone!" said Milo. "Let's do
Jakey's Greek dance. You'll have to teach us, mate!"

103

The Tweenies stood in a circle with their hands on each others' shoulders.
They copied Jake, slowly at first and then faster and faster and faster
– until they all collapsed in a heap, giggling!

Suddenly, they heard the surprise time button being pushed for a second time. The curtains swished open...

105

"Ladies and gentlemen," said Doodles,
"meet Dancing Doodles!"
Then Doodles began to dance,
and this time everyone
clapped and cheered.

The End

Rock-A-Bye Robot

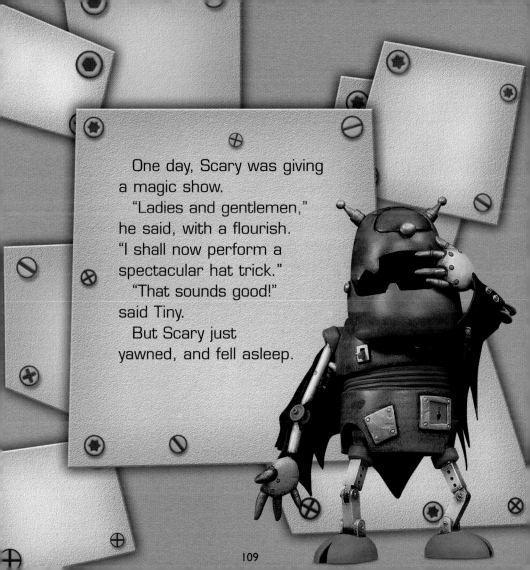

One day, Scary was giving a magic show.

"Ladies and gentlemen," he said, with a flourish. "I shall now perform a spectacular hat trick."

"That sounds good!" said Tiny.

But Scary just yawned, and fell asleep.

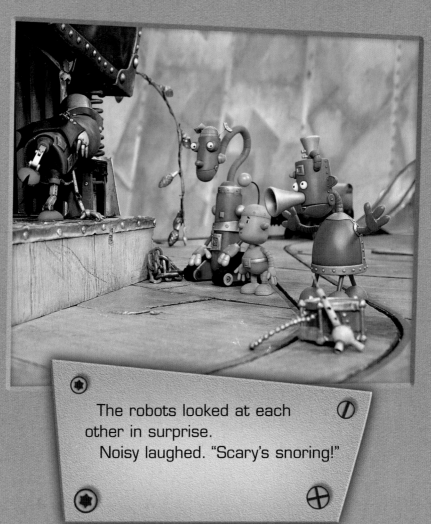

The robots looked at each other in surprise.

Noisy laughed. "Scary's snoring!"

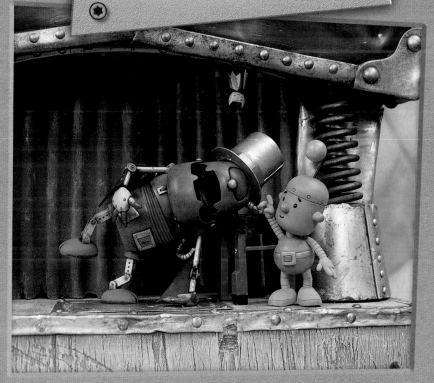

"Well, I haven't got time for this," said Stretchy, rolling off. "There's a delivery of junk due."

Tiny woke Scary. "Why are you so tired?" he asked.

Scary yawned.

"Sorry," he said. "I had a bad dream last night, and couldn't get back to sleep."

"Hmm," said Tiny.
"Why don't you sit down
on the stage and have a nap?
Noisy and I will think of something
to help you sleep tonight."

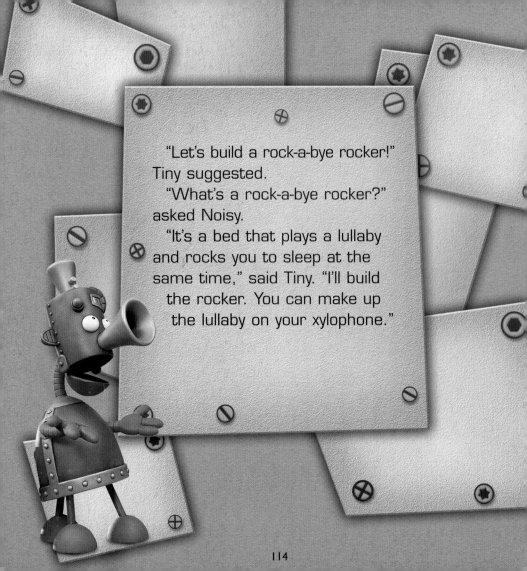

"Let's build a rock-a-bye rocker!"
Tiny suggested.

"What's a rock-a-bye rocker?"
asked Noisy.

"It's a bed that plays a lullaby
and rocks you to sleep at the
same time," said Tiny. "I'll build
the rocker. You can make up
the lullaby on your xylophone."

While Tiny and Noisy
worked, Stretchy was waiting
for his next delivery.
Suddenly, the junk chute
began to rumble.

Thump! Something furry fell out.

"Goodness me, it's a teddy!" said Stretchy. "But he's not very well."

"I know someone who
likes teddies," thought Stretchy.
He went to see Stripy.
"Hello Stripy," said Stretchy.
"Can you mend this teddy?"

"I'll try," said Stripy, gently holding the broken teddy next to his own Teddy. "I'll call him Fuzzy. Say hello to Fuzzy, Teddy."

By the end of the day, Stripy
and Teddy had mended Fuzzy...

...and Tiny and Noisy had finished the rock-a-bye rocker.

"Turning this button makes the rock-a-bye rocker move faster or slower," Tiny explained to Scary. "And this button makes the music louder or softer."

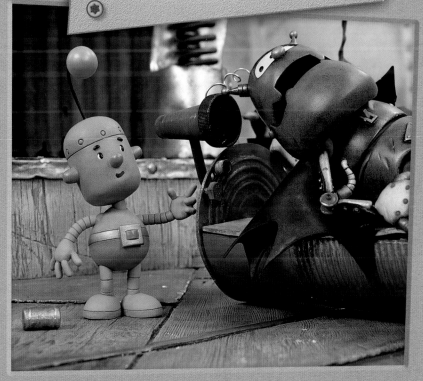

"Remarkable!" said Scary.
"Well, it's time for me to pull the Day-Night Lever," said Tiny. "So you can try the rocker right away."

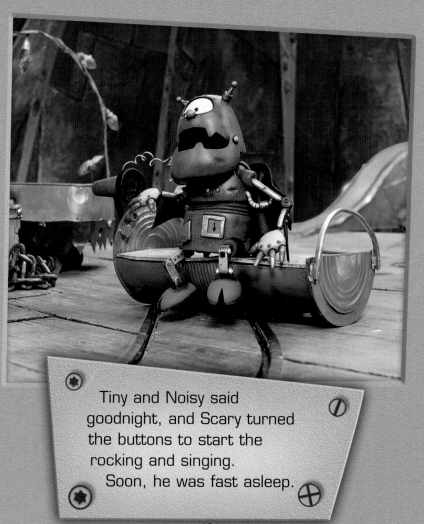

Tiny and Noisy said
goodnight, and Scary turned
the buttons to start the
rocking and singing.
   Soon, he was fast asleep.

But Flappy the bat
wasn't asleep.
    She wanted to play.
    She flew down and turned one
button. The music got louder.

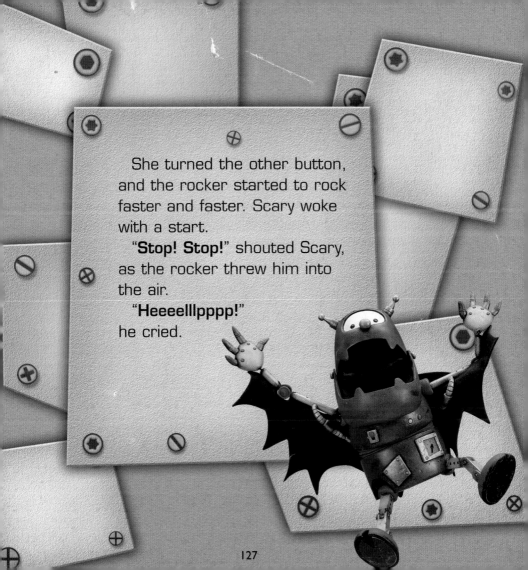

She turned the other button, and the rocker started to rock faster and faster. Scary woke with a start.

"**Stop! Stop!**" shouted Scary, as the rocker threw him into the air.

"**Heeeelllpppp!**" he cried.

Luckily for Scary, he
landed on Fuzzy.
"I say, Stripy!" said Scary.
"He's terrific. All soft and cuddly."
"He's called Fuzzy," said Stripy.

"Would you like to look after him? I already have Teddy."

Scary took Fuzzy home and stretched out to sleep on him. He slept soundly till morning.

But someone found a
use for Tiny's rock-a-bye rocker.
Flappy tied on some reins. Then
she turned the rocking up fast, and
played on the rocker all night long.

The End

Train Driver Tubb

The children had left a model train in the bathroom.

"Chuff chuff! Whoo whoo!" cried Tubb. "Benjie and Sis' train is great! All aboard!"

"I heard Benjie say that the train's very important, because it's carrying a safe full of gold!" said Sploshy.

"Is gold more important than bubbles?" asked Terence.

"Much more important, Terence," said Reg.

Terence wanted to drive the train carrying gold.
Finbar and Winona offered to help make the train noises.
But Tubb wanted to do everything himself.

"You can't drive, chuff *and* whistle," said Sploshy.

"I can!" said Tubb. "**If only** this were a real train...I'd show you could do *everything!*"

Suddenly...

"Swimmin'," said Tubb. He was a *real* driver on a *real* train!

He blew the whistle, pulled the levers, turned the
steering wheel and stoked the fire, as the little engine
chuffed down the track.

Sploshy and Reg came to help.

"No," said Tubb. "I'm in charge. You're the passengers.
This train is very special. It's carrying *real gold*!"

"Look!" said Reg, suddenly.
"Robbers! They must be after
the gold!"

139

"We're the mighty train robbers!" said Finbar.
"We've come for the gold!" said Terence.

Quickly they tied up Tubb, Sploshy and Reg.

"Hey! You can't do this!" said Tubb.

"We already have!" said Finbar.

"Hold on," said Sploshy. "I want to be a robber."
"Me, too!" said Reg.

"Come on then," said Terence, untying Sploshy and Reg.
"To the gold!"

"You won't get away with this!" said Tubb, trying to wriggle free. His foot caught a lever and it snapped off.

"Oh, no!" he gasped. "That lever controls our speed!"

"It's no good!" said Tubb, exhausted. "The train's out of control!"

The train was racing down the track.

"You have to stop the train before it gets to the bend!" cried Reg.

"We'll go off the track!"
said Terence.
    "This is mighty scary!"
said Finbar.

"I thought I could do it by myself,"
"but I can't! If we work together, we
just do it."

"No problem!" said Sploshy, and
the brake lever.

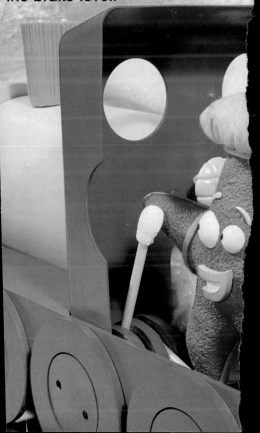

e in the boiler.

...n, until...just before the bend...

"We saved the train!" said Tubb. "How can I ever thank you?"
"Let us steal the gold!" said the robbers.
"I won't let you steal the gold," said Tubb,
"but I will share it with you."

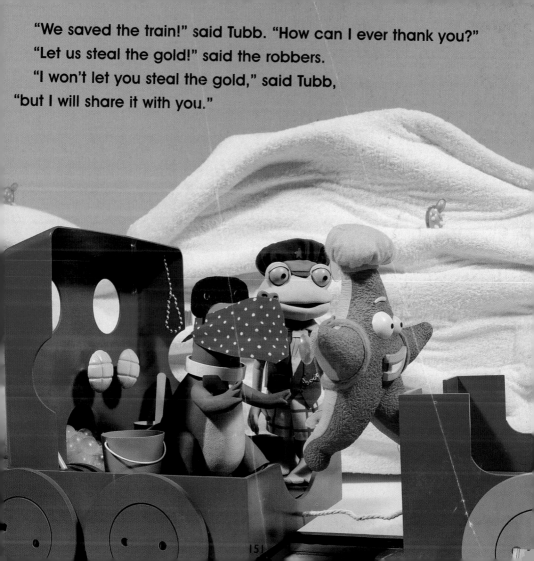

Tubb flung open the door to the safe.

"But it's empt...it's empt...there's nothing there!" said Reg.

"**If only** I'd asked someone to help me load the gold in the first place..." said Tubb.

And then...

They were all back in the bathroom, and the train was a toy.

"It's no fun playing with the train if you do *everything*, Tubb!" said Sploshy.

"Oh, I see…" said Tubb, thoughtfully. "Um…would you like to drive, Sploshy?"

"Splish splash splosh! *Yes, please!*"

But before the train could set off, Reg called out from the landing.
"Rubbadubbers! Rubbadubbers! Bathtime scramble!"
"**Swimmin'**," said Tubb. "It's bathtime!"

The End

This edition published in 2006 by:
BBC CHILDREN'S BOOKS
The Penguin Group
Penguin Books Ltd, 80 Strand, London WC2 0RL, England
Penguin Group (USA) Inc., 375 Hudson Street, New York, New York 10014, USA
Penguin Group (Australia), 250 Camberwell Road, Camberwell, Victoria 3124, Australia
(a division of Pearson Australia Group Pty Ltd)
Canada, India, New Zealand, South Africa
Penguin Books Ltd, Registered Offices: 80 Strand, London, WC2R 0RL, England
1 3 5 7 9 10 8 6 4 2
ISBN 10: 1 405 90317 1 ISBN 13: 978 1 40590317 2
Printed in China